THE NECROMANCER'S LAIR

MICHAEL KINGSWOOD

Gareth and his sworn man, Hatherle, delve into the lair of a Necromancer who has been terrorizing the surrounding territory, seeking the reward on his head.

But trips, traps, puzzles, and the dead themselves serve as the Necromancer's guards, making this the most dangerous mission Gareth has ever taken on.

Enjoy the book! After you're done, please come to Michael's website and sign up for his mailing list at michaelkingswood.com/newsletter-signup/. Guaranteed to be spam free, he uses it to announce new releases and special promotions for his fans.

❧ I ❧

Gareth's chest heaved as he sucked in gulps of air. His heart pounded in his ears, and he tingled all over with a mixture of exhilaration and fear. He leapt backwards, leaving grimy claws to scratch harmlessly along the front of his steel breastplate before he got out of reach.

This thing was relentless! Gareth had hit it a dozen times before, each blow of his axe tearing out large bits of flesh and muscle, but it kept on coming. Even losing an arm did not stop it.

The creature shambled forward, the putrid scent of rotting flesh leading the way. Its mouth lolled open in a brainless snarl and its eyes shown with a ghostly light that did not come close to resembling life. And yet it moved. Ragged cloths, the last remains of its funeral raiment, Gareth was sure, still clung to its body in places, but were at best an afterthought. If such a thing as this had any thoughts at all.

Gareth drew a deep breath and adjusted his grip on the handle of his axe. He wondered for a heartbeat how much longer he could keep hacking at the thing before it simply wore him down from fatigue.

Then it was on him. The nails—claws—of its sole remaining arm thrust toward Gareth's throat. It was an awkward attack, as clumsy as the thing's stride, and Gareth easily sidestepped it. He gritted his teeth and, with a grunt that was nearly a shout, brought his axe down.

The thing's arm went flying, cut off at the elbow.

No blood flowed; there was none remaining in its body. Neither did the thing seem to feel pain, or slow. It stumbled forward, turning to face him, before launching itself straight at him, its rotting teeth its last weapon.

Except for the stink. It became overpowering as the thing's mouth drew near. Gareth nearly gagged, only years of training stopping him from losing his composure.

Would the thing never die?

He recoiled and struck again with his axe.

The half-moon of steel struck the beast in the forehead, cleaving its head nearly in two before lodging in place.

The light in the creature's eyes flickered and it shambled forward another half-step. Then the light went out completely and it fell forward. It hit the ground with a sickening, squishy thud, and lay still.

"Ye Gods," Gareth muttered as he wiped his brow with the back of his hand. He took a deep breath and had to stop himself from shuddering.

"Well fought, my lord," said Hatherle from behind him, "but if I may make a suggestion?"

Gareth scowled and looked over his shoulder.

The slender man behind him and to his left was less armored than he was; just a leather breastplate, mostly hidden by the dark grey tunic he wore over top. His pants were light brown, tight-fitting, and tucked into calf-high turned-down boots. He wore a pack on his back, and a grey scull cap covered most of his head, leaving just a few strands of his blond hair falling out. His hands rested upon the pommel of his longsword, which he held point-down into the dirt before him.

"What?"

Hatherle cleared his throat. "I would avoid flesh wounds for such as these," he nodded toward the still corpse at his feet - its head was severed from its body, "and go for the head instead."

Gareth stared at him for a long moment, then rolled his eyes, bent over, and grabbed the haft of his axe. "No kidding." The axe was stuck fast. This was going to take a bit of work. He stepped over the rotting corpse and took hold with both hands. "You could have helped, you know, if you figured it out so fast."

Gareth practically heard Hatherle's shrug. "You seemed to have things well in hand, my lord."

Gareth heaved upward, his breath leaving his lungs in a long grunt as he strained against the axe handle. For a long several seconds, nothing happened. Then, without warning, the axe came free. Gareth stumbled backwards, almost tripping over the creature's severed forearm. Decaying corpse-matter of some variety or other—Gareth did not want to think about what it was exactly—sprayed out of the thing's head where his axe used to be.

He shuddered, trying not to inhale the newly-increased stench.

Instead, he turned away and stalked further into the cave, pausing only to remove a rag from behind his belt. He wiped the blade of his axe clean of slime, bone, and the rest, as he walked.

Hatherle followed.

"I asked you to stop calling me that. I'm no lord," Gareth growled over his shoulder.

Again with the semi-audible shrug. "Lord Hadley offered a title to whomever rids the county of the Necromancer, so I expect you will be soon. Besides, I am sworn to your service, my lord. What else should I call you?"

Gareth ground his teeth. They had argued this point several times before, and he had never been able to get Hatherle to budge. Best to just let it lie.

"What do you make of those things?"

"Necromancers *are* masters of all things dead, my Lord. Considering our quest - "

"Yes, I know. I just meant, what do you think about them?"

There was a long pause. "My lord?"

Nevermind.

The reanimated corpses were clearly watchdogs. That meant Gareth's notion was right: there was a passage from the cave into the Necromancer's tower. Hatherle either really did not see it or was just playing dumb because that was what he thought a man servant was supposed to do with his Lord. It would be less annoying if he was consistent about it, if the later.

The light was beginning to fade. Gareth took a moment to look back.

The cave mouth was about twenty-five feet behind them. The jagged rocks around its entrance really did make it look like a mouth, come to think of it. The floor of the cave was relatively flat, littered here and there with rocks and boulders...and two hacked-up corpses. But as far as caves went, it was easy to navigate.

Looking back to the passage ahead, the cave bent around to the left. Very soon the light from the entrance would be gone.

"Break out the torches," he said.

Hatherle nodded acquiescence and took off his pack. He spent a moment digging around before coming up with two of the torches they had made back in town.

Gareth set his axe down and took out flint and steel. Hatherle held the torches out toward him, and he began to work. In a few moments, both torches were alight, and the two men set off once more.

"Keep a close eye out," Gareth said softly, receiving only a short grunt in return.

Glancing aside, Gareth noted an expression of annoyance on Hatherle's face that disappeared as soon as the other man felt his eyes on him. He had to suppress a grin; it was not often that Hatherle let his facade crack.

The cave continued to twist to the left and ascended. It gradually became more narrow, and the ceiling lowered as well. The small pools of light cast by their torches only heightened the sense that the world was slowly closing in on them. Gareth felt the hair on his arms stand on end and he began to get a queasy feeling in his stomach. He had to force himself to breath normally, but nonetheless he felt a deepening pressure on his chest. He had never cared for tight spaces.

Finally, the passage leveled, though it became noticeably more rough, with more rounded boulders strew hither and yon, along with the occasional stalactite and stalagmite. Then there was a whisper of moving air. Gareth would not have noticed it except for the stillness of the rest of the cave. The slight breeze carried with it the odor of dampness, with a hint of corruption beneath.

Gareth rolled his shoulders, settling the shield he kept slung on his back a bit more comfortably. Then, flexing his fingers on the haft of his axe, he stepped around a particularly large boulder.

And found himself flailing his arms to keep from falling as his foot came down on only empty air. Only Hatherle's quick reaction, grabbing his shoulder and hauling him back, prevented disaster.

Shivering from a surge of adrenalin, Gareth exhaled deeply and nodded thanks. Hatherle returned the nod, but said nothing. His eyes said enough. Gareth needed to be more careful. It would not do for Hatherle to lose his Lord this quickly into his tenure as Gareth's sworn man. Gareth managed not to scowl at the man before he turned back to the fall that had almost taken him.

His heart sank.

The floor dropped away on the other side of the boulder, becoming a sheer crevasse that descended farther than the torch's light could reach. The crack ran in both directions as far as he could see and was about fifteen feet wide, too far to jump. Except for a narrow ledge leading off to the left on his side of the crevasse, there was no way forward.

"That is discouraging," Hatherle said as he eyed the crack.

"That's one way to say it. I didn't see any branching passages or anything that looked like a door. Did you?"

Hatherle shook his head.

Gareth sighed and stepped to the left left-hand wall, where the ledge lay. It was about two feet wide and proceeded on for quite some distance, well past the illumination from the torches. It was not a very inviting route.

"I'm not sure I like the notion of sliding along that ledge, but I don't see any other way to go," Gareth said. He glanced back at Hatherle. "What do you think?"

The slender man shrugged. "I go where you go, my Lord."

Great help, that one.

Gareth sighed. "All right. Let's go."

With a deep breath, he inched his foot out onto the ledge.

It was too narrow to walk properly, not without great risk of overbalancing and falling, so he pressed his back against the cave wall and slid along sideways. It was slow going, and awkward. Very quickly in the process, he switched his axe to his left hand—the one that was leading the way—and the torch into his right. At least he would have a chance of defending himself that way, and he was not staring directly into the torch's flame.

At one point, Gareth's foot came down on the very lip of the ledge, and part of it broke away. He pressed himself back more tightly against the wall, expecting the rest of the ledge to fall away beneath him at any moment. The various prayers that he had not spoken since he was a boy flew through his mind as he awaited the end, and he felt a cold sweat beading on his brow.

But the rest of the ledge held. After a long moment, Hatherle cleared his throat, rousing Gareth from his near-panicked state. He shook himself and blinked, then managed a rueful grin and continued on.

Finally, after what felt like forever, but was probably only a few hundred feet, the wall expanded back into an oblong alcove that almost appeared carved out of the rock face, it was so smooth. About twenty feet deep and half again as many wide, the walls were rounded, rising to meet in a sort of dome in the center of the alcove area. Aside from that, however, the alcove was unremarkable.

And empty.

The walls were bare rock, with no protuberances, the floor smooth and level. Even the ledge did not continue beyond the alcove.

This was it. End of the road.

"Damnit," Gareth muttered. "I thought sure there was a way."

"The presence of our previous adversaries certainly suggested as much, my Lord," Hatherle replied. "Though I hesitate to imagine beings like those successfully navigating that ledge."

Gareth was forced to nod in agreement. He had been wondering that himself as they crept down the ledge; those walking corpses were not particularly nimble. How had they managed to not fall off the ledge? Of course, there was nothing to stop the Necromancer from simply bringing them in through the cave mouth.

By why go to all the effort to do so if the only thing in the cave was...*this*?

"There's got to be more here than meets the eye," Gareth said. "Take left, Hatherle. I'll start on the right. We'll meet in the middle."

He did not wait for the man servant to respond, but strode over to the far end of the alcove. Moving slowly, he tapped the flat of his axe against the cave wall. A metallic "tink" rang out, almost eclipsing the softer ring of the stone as the metal touched it. Not particularly melodious, but true - the wall was solid there.

Gareth continued in that manner, ranging up and down the wall at random as he eased his way around the alcove, until he met Hatherle halfway around, as planned.

"Anything?"

The man servant just shrugged. "Sounds solid to me, my lord."

"Hmmph."

Gareth frowned at the stone wall for a long moment, his thoughts whirling. He had been so sure! The wasted time and effort rankled, but more than that the thought that another may have already breached the Tower's walls ahead of him drove a spike of irritation that bordered on rage into him.

"If I may suggest..."

"Stow it, Hatherle!" Gareth could not keep himself from shouting.

Hatherle blanched and drew back on himself, his already slight frame seeming to shrivel as he recoiled from his Lord's anger.

His Lord.

Gareth had no claim to that title. Nor did he want one. Why would the little fellow not listen when he explained that? It was almost enough to bring the rage full-on for a moment.

Then Gareth got ahold of himself, forced himself back to calm. Or at least just more-than-mild irritation. He knew exactly why Hatherle had sworn to him, why he called Gareth his Lord.

And Gareth did not have the heart to force that devotion from him.

He drew a deep breath and forced the last of his anger away. "I'm sorry, Hatherle," he said, making his tone as kind as he could.

Hatherle blinked. He actually looked confused. "No need to apologize, my Lord. I serve at your pleasure."

How to explain? The issue almost made Gareth angry again, but he was back in control. "Nevermind. Let's go. We'll take the short, direct way. Straight through the front door." He barked out a laugh that he hoped sounded confident. "That ol' Necromancer will never expect something like that."

Gareth turned and walked back toward the ledge, his earlier trepidation about taking it forgotten, at least for the moment. The sound of Hatherle clearing his throat brought him to a halt.

Gareth looked back at Hatherle over his shoulder. "What?"

Hatherle gave the slightest of shrugs. "I go where you go, my Lord, but..."

"Out with it, man."

Hatherle frowned. "Not to contradict you, but I suspect the Necromancer expects that very thing. He counts on it, and has his defenses arrayed against it. The odds of success, or even survival, in a frontal assault are..."

"Never tell me the odds."

Hatherle's teeth clacked together and he managed a rueful smile. "Pardon, my Lord. I forgot."

Gareth looked at the slender man servant for half a minute, then rolled his eyes and threw up his hands. "Well what do you suggest?"

"My Lord, I would not presume..."

Gareth's stare carried daggers. Hatherle's speech slowed and came to a halt beneath its weight. Finally, he made a vague gesture toward the top of the ceiling, where the dome reached its zenith.

Gareth frowned and walked over to the center of the alcove. As he stepped beneath the ceiling's zenith, it was like a key turning in a lock. He suddenly saw what Hatherly was referring to. Standing exactly there, the patterns of the rock came together and formed a sigil of a wolf biting the neck of a fallen deer, the sigil of the Necromancer Gareth presumed. The wolf's eyes were open. They stared behind Gareth and to his right...toward the stone floor.

Gareth turned around and looked down toward where the wolf was gazing. There, he saw a circle surrounding a five-pointed star inlaid into the ground.

He felt his eyes going wide as his jaw dropped. "Hatherle," he began. Then he caught himself as a realization hit him. He rounded on the slender man, his earlier anger rekindled. "You knew?"

Hatherle shook his head. "I saw the sigil in the ceiling, yes..."

"Why the hell didn't you say anything?" Gareth felt his heart rate beginning to climb.

"I was sure you would find it, my Lord." He smiled, his face becoming pure admiration and devotion. "It was not my place to interrupt."

Gareth bit back a curse, instead grinding his teeth to keep a vicious tongue-lashing from spewing forth. He glared at Hatherle for a minute - the man did not have the grace to look embarrassed - then sighed and looked back at the star and circle on the ground.

"Well...what do you make of this?"

Hatherle walked up next to Gareth, his expression curious. When he stopped beneath the sigil on the ceiling and followed Gareth's pointing finger with his gaze, his eyes widened.

"I did not see that, my Lord," he began. His lips pursed together. "Interesting. As you well know, that symbol is used by magicians and wizards everywhere, as the center of a summoning circle."

Gareth knew no such thing, but he did know better than to interrupt when Hatherle went on a tear. He nodded, putting on an encouraging grin - or at least one he hoped was encouraging. But Hatherle seemed not to notice as he kept right on talking.

"The symbol's power constrains the beings the wizard summons, allows him a certain amount of control during the meeting." Hatherle's tongue clicked behind his front teeth. "I suspect a Necromancer would be especially comfortable with this symbol. The dead are...quite unhappy...when disturbed." He cleared his throat. "Or so I hear."

Gareth supposed Hatherle's last comment made sense. Sort of.

"So now we know the Necromancer was here at some point." Gareth left the area beneath the ceiling's zenith and stepped toward the symbol on the floor.

He half expected the symbol to fade from his vision when he left the zenith, but it did not. It was as though once unlocked, the symbols were easily seen.

On a hunch, he looked back at the zenith. The wolf sigil was still there. Yep, whatever it was that had prevented him from seeing it before was gone.

Gareth wished that did not make him feel so frightened.

He crouched down and examined the symbol. From up close, it almost appeared to be etched into the floor. But that did not make any sense; if it had been, he would have seen it before. Setting his axe down, he ran his fingers along the symbol. Sure enough, the lines of the star and circle were recessed into the stone of the floor.

"I'll be damned," Gareth murmured.

"I should hope not, my Lord."

Hatherle's ears were entirely too keen sometimes. Rather than respond, Gareth just grunted and went back to examining the symbol. The edges of the lines were abrupt, hardly weathered at all. Which was not surprising considering how little traffic came through this cave. All the same, that meant they had been made relatively recently.

Gareth traced out the lines of the symbol again, more slowly. There was something...

"Well how about that?" Gareth looked up at Hatherle. "The engraving is a bit deeper at each point of the star, see?"

Hatherle frowned slightly and crouched down next to Gareth. After a moment, he nodded.

"Indeed, my Lord. And it looks like there is something embedded within, as well."

Gareth blinked and lowered his head to examine the points of the star more closely. As he did so, he moved the torch, now back in his left hand, and he saw a glint of reflected light from one of the points.

"Is that metal?"

Hatherle shrugged. "It does appear so, my Lord."

Gareth bit his lip in thought for a moment. This

was becoming more and more interesting. Clearly the necromancer had left this symbol here, and gone to no small amount of effort to do so. Maybe...

"Maybe it's like a doorknob," he said, voicing his thoughts aloud.

Hatherle shrugged again, but did not reply.

Gareth glanced at him and sighed. Sometimes the man's penchant for speaking his thoughts became annoying, but he was knowledgable about many things; scholars and sages were useful that way. But he seemed to pick the strangest times to go silent, and that was almost *more* annoying.

"Back up, Hatherle. I'm going to try something, and I have no idea what it's going to do."

"As you wish, my Lord." The slender man stood and moved over to the wall. Gareth noted he was right near the ledge, no doubt ready to make a quick escape if things went badly wrong.

Smart man.

"Here goes nothing."

Gareth kept a dagger sheathed on his belt, opposite the iron ring that he slung the haft of his axe through when he did not want to carry it. He withdrew the dagger, hardly noticing the familiar sound of steel drawing across hardened leather, and paused.

Where to begin? There were no markings to make any one point of the star more important than another. No indication of where to start and where to end. If Gareth had put this little contraption together, he would make sure to have something horrible happen to a person who did not execute it correctly. It only made sense the Necromancer would have done the same.

But there was no way to know that without trying, was there?

"I am a sodding fool," he muttered, then he

pressed the tip of his dagger into the lower right point on the star.

Scarlet light, somehow beautiful despite its unearthly hue, began shining from the point as soon as the steel of the dagger made contact. The glow continued after Gareth removed the dagger, but nothing untoward occurred. He must be on the right track; he was not dead.

Yet.

Moving with careful slowness, he pressed the tip of the dagger into the remaining four points of the star. Each time, the points began glowing just as the first one did. As he removed the dagger from the final point, Gareth felt a certain satisfaction, and he grinned. Turns out this little riddle was not so difficult, after all.

He rocked back on his heels and his grin faded. The points of light were dimmer...or was that his imagination?

No, they *were* dimmer. What...

The lights went out.

"Dammit! What the hell just happened?"

Hatherle was next to him again; Gareth had not noticed his approach, so caught up in the moment he had been. He had to resist the urge to slap himself. That was the sort of carelessness that could get them both killed.

"I suspect," Hatherle began, rubbing at his chin with the fingers of his left hand, "that you are correct about this device's purpose, my Lord. It may well open a portal of some sort. But it will need to work as a whole, not as a collection of individual parts."

Gareth blinked. "Come again?"

Hatherle gave him a look that said he was missing the forest for the trees. "The star is a series of lines, not a set of five points."

The realization hit Gareth in a flash. Idiot! He

should not have needed Hatherle to come to that conclusion.

Grumbling, Gareth thrust the tip of his dagger into the lower right point on the star. This time, he did not remove the dagger but instead traced the star out, line by line and point by point, until he had completed the entire thing. As he did, the glow began from the first point, then continued down the line to the second, getting brighter as it went. By the time he was tracing out the line between the fourth and fifth points, the glow was bright enough that he had to squint to avoid being dazzled.

Done! Gareth pulled his dagger from the engraving, and the circle began glowing on its own, a blue glow this time that complimented the star's crimson but also added to the glare so much that he had to look away.

He saw Hatherle, shielding his eyes with a raised hand, a look of surprised awe on his face.

Then the light flicked out, leaving them both in blackness.

At first, Gareth thought he was blind. The light, as bright as it was, had overcome him completely; he had turned away too slowly, and he was doomed to live out the rest of his life in darkness, begging passersby for whatever coins or scraps they deigned to share with him.

It was almost enough to make him open a vein with the dagger in his hand.

After a minute or so, however, he realized he could see. Ever so slightly. There was a light, extremely faint, streaming in from somewhere, off to his right, he thought. It was difficult to tell, because the light was so dim he almost thought he was imagining it, at first.

Once, when Gareth was young, he had locked himself inside a padded chest while playing hide and seek. He had almost died of suffocation before his parents finally found him, but while he waited, he experienced near total silence. The padding of the chest blocked the outside noise so well he could not hear anything. After a short while, he began imagining he heard things: dogs barking, laughter, whispers...the sort of faint whispers that would drive a man mad if he listened to them for too long.

The light he experienced now reminded him of that day, and he felt a cold shiver of fear run down his spine. Swallowing to repress the bile he knew would try to come up if he let it, he pushed himself to his feet.

"Hatherle," Gareth said, trying hard to not let his sudden fear show in his tone. "Are you still there?"

There was silence for a long moment, then a discontented snort announced the man servant's presence. "Here, my Lord. That was...most instructive." Hatherle normally was extremely pleased to learn something, remnants of his old profession, no doubt. Not this time. He sounded positively chagrined.

Not that Gareth felt much better. Sheathing his dagger, he peered around, trying to get his bearings, and failed.

Then, all at once, he realized he still felt grainy wood in his left hand - the torch. He had not extinguished it; why was it not shining?

Gingerly, Gareth raised his right hand to the end of the torch, where the flame should have been. He felt no heat, even when he closed his hand around it. The top of the torch crumbled, ash falling away where the fuel and underlying wood had burned, but aside from that he would never have been able to tell the thing had ever been lit, as cool as it was.

"What the..."

"It would seem," Hatherle said, "that our query is a bit more clever than you gave him credit for." There was a brief pause before he added, "My Lord." Clearly he was re-thinking his pledge of service. Or he was just annoyed because he did not see this turn of events coming. Gareth would not give odds either way.

"Wonderful." Gareth tossed the torch, useless now, to the ground, then crouched back down and felt around until he found his axe.

Feeling a bit better with the weapon's solid weight in his right hand, he stood back up and shrugged his shield off his back, then slipped it onto his left forearm.

What was making that light? Gareth turned his head left and right, but no matter which way he looked, it was all the same. Just darkness illuminated by the faintest hint of light, just enough to remind him he was not blind. He could find no source, see no details.

But there had to be something there.

He rolled his shoulders and straightened - he found himself hunching over without realizing it, an instinctual response to the oppressing gloom no doubt. "Hatherle, grab the back of my belt."

He did not wait for the other man to respond. He just stepped forward, trusting in Hatherle's seemingly instinctive need to obey. Gareth felt a reassuring tug on his belt as he moved forward; Hatherle had grabbed on before it was too late.

One direction was as good as another, so he continued forward in as straight a line as he could manage. It would be very easy to get turned around with no visual reference, but there was nothing else to it. And he had always been good at walking along logs, even with his eyes closed. Sooner or later, if he kept straight enough, he had to run into something.

Sure enough, he did exactly that. One moment he was walking slowly forward. The next, he found himself falling, his outstretched foot having come down on nothing but thin air. The cry of chagrin behind him, and the desperate tugging at the back of his belt, told him that Hatherle, too, had fallen, but he had only enough time to throw his axe aside—it would not do to land on it and impale himself—before he struck ground. Hard.

A heartbeat later, Hatherle landed atop him.

Gareth's breath left his lungs in a rush, and the momentary lack of breath clouded his other pains for a time. Finally, when he was able to inhale again, he took stock.

He hurt all over; he had landed flat on his belly, spreading the impact all over his body. A small mercy, that. Had he landed any other way, he would likely be nursing one or more broken bones. But after a short consideration, Gareth decided he would have bruises pretty much everywhere. But he was functional. If that was the right word for it.

"Get off me," he said, his voice harsher than he intended it between his aches and difficulty breathing.

It was only after Hatherle rolled off and Gareth forced himself up onto his hands and knees that he realized he could see again. Or rather, that the light was bright enough that he could make out his surroundings without difficulty.

He almost wished he could not.

He and Hatherle sat in a small room, maybe ten feet on a side. Although room was probably a misnomer. All around him were steel bars, beyond which he could make out little of the chamber beyond. The floor was rock, as was the ceiling. And how did that work exactly? He could see no hint of the hole he fell through, though it must have been there.

"Bugger me," he breathed.

He looked around again. Whether it was because the light grew more bright or because his eyes were becoming more accustomed to it, he found he could see the chamber housing his cell a bit better. It was made of stone, chiseled blocks that fit together tightly enough that he wondered whether the builders had bothered with mortar, and was empty save for their cell.

And his axe, lying about five feet beyond the bars of the cell, off to the right.

"Bugger me," he said again, more emphatically.

"Not even if you paid me, my Lord," said Hatherle as he pushed himself to his feet. He took a moment to brush himself off, smoothing his clothing at the same time, as he looked around. "Well," he said, "this is rather...discouraging."

He had a way with words, Hatherle did.

								❧ 3 ❧

It was difficult to tell how much time passed with no external reference. But regardless, they remained stuck in that small cell for far too long.

At first, Gareth plotted ways to escape. They could team up to bend a bar out of shape and then Hatherle, the thinner of the two, could slip out and figure out how to free Gareth. Hatherle could stand on Gareth's shoulders and work the stone where it encased the bars with Gareth's dagger. Given enough time and effort, he would surely be able to remove enough stone that Gareth could knock a couple bars out.

In truth, Gareth was surprised Hatherle went along with those ideas, oaths or no. Regardless, it did not work. Nothing worked.

And so they sat idly, letting time pass by as they steadily grew more thirsty and hungry, and as fatigue began to set in. Those sensations, and the urgings of nature, were the only way to measure time's passage. It must surely have been a day, maybe more, before their captor revealed himself.

All at once, the seemingly unbroken wall of the chamber housing their cell became...broken. A portion of the wall swung open, like a door. Except before it swung open there was no indication of hinges or any break in the stone at all. In fact, the "door" bisected several of the stones that made up the walls of the chamber.

A rush of air accompanied the door's opening, bringing with it a sickly-sweet odor that Gareth could not quite place. It was familiar, but...off, somehow. His contemplation of the odor was short-lived though, his attention being taken by the man who stepped delicately into the chamber.

Delicate summed the man up perfectly. Hatherle was slender. This fellow made him look like a hulking slab of muscle. Gareth was not entirely certain how he managed to support his own weight, let alone the weight of the black robes he wore. They were cowled, the robes, though he wore the hood thrown back, and were cinched around his waist by a length of red-brown cloth of some sort. The man's features were sharp, almost skeletal, which was fitting in a way, but far from weak. His dark eyes peered at Gareth and Hatherle intensely from beneath narrow black brows that matched the short-cut black hair atop his head.

The Necromancer, Gareth presumed. Of course, the shambling figures of two reanimated dead men that accompanied him on either side as he strode into the room would have given that away even if he did not look the part.

"Welcome, friends," said the Necromancer. His voice was surprising: deep and strong, belonging to a much more substantial man. And cultured. Gareth had encountered Lords who spoke with less precision and elegance than this man. No simple power-hungry lunatic, this one.

"Glad to be here," Gareth replied, trying to keep his tone steady despite the shiver crawling up his spine.

The Necromancer smirked slightly. "I've no doubt." He stopped his approach about ten feet from the cell. The walking corpses halted as well as he crossed his arms over his chest. "You are the first to stumble upon my back door," he said. "The others all tried a more...direct route." He made a vague gesture toward the corpse on the left. Gareth followed the gesture with his gaze and found his bowels turning to liquid. He knew that man.

Man. Hard to call him that now. But Ranulf had been powerful, jolly, and loyal once. To see him standing there, barely recognizable from the decay of his flesh even as the Necromancer's ghastly art kept him from his rest, nearly unmanned Gareth.

He had not known Ranulf had sought to challenge the Necromancer; he had simply stopped coming to the pub one day. Gareth assumed he had just moved on, or found a different watering hole. Though why he would not have at least said goodbye to those he had become friendly with stung a bit.

Apparently Gareth had been wrong, and that error filled him with fear.

If such a mighty man as Ranulf could not defeat the Necromancer, what chance did *he* have? Especially considering the circumstances.

He kept his mouth shut. Better to let the Necromancer speak. Perhaps he would give something away.

"What did you hope to accomplish?" The Necromancer's tone was conversational, though tainted with a hint of derision.

Gareth shrugged and spread his hands. "Do you really need to ask?"

Amusement flashed through the Necromancer's eyes, and he shook his head. "No, I suppose not. I am, after all, *the great menace*. The *threat to all humanity*." He took on an ironic, almost mocking tone as he emphasized those last words.

There was a moment of silence as the Necromancer just looked at Gareth. Then he sighed and shook his head. "Does it never occur to any of you that I might have a good reason for my studies?"

He did not wait for Gareth's response. He just turned away and strode back through the doorway. "A pity," he said, and made a circular gesture with his right hand.

Then he was gone, but the animated corpses remained.

Gareth blinked. "Um...ok..."

A sharp crack from overhead drew Gareth's gaze to the ceiling, and he leapt backwards, pushing himself off the ground with a powerful spring of his legs. He did not go far before slamming into the bars behind him with a loud CLANG of steel striking steel. Had he not been wearing his breastplate, the impact would have hurt. A lot.

But the ceiling stone coming dislodged and falling down right where he was standing would have hurt a lot more.

Hatherle, too, dove to the side. He hit the ground and rolled to his feet to Gareth's left, his eyes wide.

"My lord," he began.

"Yes, I know. We're in trouble. I'm working on it."

Hatherle shook his head vigorously, his eyes locked on the ceiling, where the block used to be. "No, my lord...look!"

Gareth looked back up, and his heart sank. Hands were reaching through the hole left by the block that had just fallen. Rotting, dead hands, with the flesh hanging in strips from them like so many torn rags. They scrabbled around, blindly for all Gareth could tell, until they reaching the next block over. They began tugging at it.

The block, slightly larger than the one that had just fallen, had to have weighed a quarter of a ton. There was no way those dead limbs could move such a piece of stone.

Yet they did.

Slowly at first, then more quickly with each passing second, the stone began to rock. Dirt and dust fell from around its edges: a trickle at first, then a steady stream as the block came, inexorably, free.

Gareth shuffled to the side to avoid being crushed as the second block came down, Hatherle following suit.

This was not good. Not good at all. If the falling blocks did not do them in, Gareth did not want to think about how easily such strong arms could tear he and Hatherle limb from limb if the creatures opted to come down and join them. And his axe lay out of reach, at Ranulf's corpse's feet!

Gareth took a second to wonder why Ranulf and the other corpse had stayed behind, if the intention was to crush or bludgeon he and Hatherle to death. Then he had to leap forward to avoid yet another block.

By then the ceiling was more a dark, gaping hole than anything else. Dark as it was, though, he could see the walking corpses shambling around toward their next project. Hear their unnatural silence—the lack of breath and speech—beneath the sounds of their movement. Smell the stink of their advanced state of decay, a stink so strong he could almost taste it.

Adrenalin prevented bile from rising in his throat despite the surge of revulsion he felt. Time enough for that sort of thing later. Now was for figuring out how to survive.

The hands appeared again, tugging at yet another block. But this one was next to the first block that fell.

Gareth dropped his shield to the ground, hopped up onto the fallen block, and reached up. With the added height from his perch, a pair of rotting wrists were easy to reach. He grabbed and pulled, twisting his torso to add more force to the movement. For a heartbeat, there was resistance, then the moving corpse came free and fell, and he spun completely around, to hurl it across the cell.

Toward Hatherle.

"Hatherle," he roared as he threw.

The corpse landed at the serving man's feet and moved quickly to right itself. But not quickly enough. Hatherle's sword took its head off in one smooth cut. The corpse collapsed in a heap.

Hatherle glanced at Gareth, his expression, for once, openly impressed. "Well played, my Lord," he said simply.

Gareth grinned in reply, then reached up for the next set of hands.

❀ 4 ❀

The five corpses in the ceiling managed to drop two more blocks before Gareth and Hatherle killed them all.

Again.

They never even tried to change their tactic, but simply kept on tugging and digging as Gareth pulled them down one by one. Hatherle proved efficient at dispatching them, though the last two required Gareth's intervention as well, as much due to the limited room to maneuver with all the fallen stone as anything else.

But finally, the last of the corpses lay at Gareth and Hatherle's feet. Gareth drew in a deep breath and wiped sweat from his brow, then stepped over to Hatherle and clapped him on the shoulder.

"Well done, Hatherle. We may just make it out of this yet."

No sooner had the words left his mouth when a metallic clang followed by the groan of metal being stressed beyond its capacity caused Gareth to turn around.

Ranulf and the other re-animated corpse the Necromancer left behind, a man who in life had been even larger and stronger than Ranulf from the look of him, stood right up next to the bars of the cell. Between them, they held an exceptionally stout iron rod, which they had thrust between two of the bars making up the cell's walls.

The two corpses pulled on the rod. Hard. The bars of the cell groaned in protest again and slowly bent outward.

"Oh no," Gareth breathed.

The Necromancer's reason for leaving them was plain: they were his backup plan in case the ceiling corpses failed. Gareth felt his eyes growing wide as his grin of triumph, which he wore so briefly, faded. His mouth suddenly dry, he glanced away from the two powerful corpses toward where his axe lay, so close but yet so far.

If only he could get to it, they might have a chance.

"My lord," Hatherle began as though he intended to say more, but when Gareth looked at him, the serving man was pale, his eyes wide as well. He stared at the massive corpses as they worked at the cell bars and it was plain that, for once, he was not referring to Gareth when he said Lord, but instead to his personal deity.

Gareth could not blame him for that. A few choice prayers came to mind, the ones he had recalled back on the ledge and more. He quickly shoved them away. If they were to get through this, he needed his wits, not meaningless words spoken to a being that might not even exist.

The bars were bending more quickly now, their groans of protest becoming more pronounced. Dust puffed down from the ceiling where the bars were driven in. Very soon either the bars themselves or the mortar holding them in place, if any, would give way, leaving a space that the corpses could squeeze in to.

Or a space that Gareth could exit.

It was a long shot, but there was no choice. He bent over and picked up his shield, then strapped it back onto his left forearm. "Get ready," he said, glancing at Hatherle over his shoulder. "When those bars go, we charge."

Hatherle looked at him as though he were daft. He might have a point there.

"Are you with me, Hatherle?"

The slender man hesitated then, licking his lips nervously, nodded.

It only took another minute or so, then with a final scream first one bar then the other reached the end its endurance and snapped. The top half of each clattered to the ground, falling free from their ceiling holes. The lower halves remained fixed in the holes in the floor, but bent over as they were it would be only a small challenge to vault past them.

The corpses released their great pry bar and it too clattered to the floor.

Ranulf stepped forward, his hands lifting, revealing fingers that had decayed enough that the tips were better called bony claws than anything else. The unearthly glow in his eyes dimmed as his eyelids, somehow still intact despite the decay of the rest of his body, narrowed.

Gareth had seen that expression on the powerful man before, in life. He was readying himself for a fight.

A new chill of terror swept over Gareth. How much of a man's personality, his experience, his...self remained when he became undead? Did Ranulf know what had happened to him?

If he did...the man Gareth had known would have viewed this sort of existence with revulsion, horror. Did he reside, even now, within his own skull, screaming for release yet powerless to bring it about or resist the commands of the Necromancer?

"Not me," Gareth said between barred teeth. "I'll not go like that."

Ranulf stepped forward, into the gap between the broken bars.

Gareth drew a deep breath and forced his fear down with the fiercest battle roar he could muster, then he raised his shield in front of himself and charged.

Behind him, he thought he heard Hatherle take up his own roar as he followed. Then there was only the stink of Ranulf's corpse as Gareth lowered his head and raised his shield a bit further. He struck Ranulf in the midriff. The impact was more than he expected and he almost lost his feet. For a moment he got a sinking feeling in his belly as he thought sure the large corpse would resist the attack.

Then, abruptly, Ranulf fell backwards and Gareth found himself following. It would not do to get into a wrestling match, so Gareth tucked his shoulder as he struck the floor next to the fallen corpse. He rolled with the momentum of his fall, trying to put distance between himself and his foe.

He almost succeeded.

Gareth rolled to his feet and turned, looking for his axe. It should be right here...

Then something grabbed his ankle and pulled. Hard. He lost his balance and fell to the ground before he could even begin to resist the pull. Unprepared as he was, he struck the ground hard, and once again found himself struggling to draw breath as the air left his lungs.

The noise of his armor striking the stone rang in his ears, stunning him almost as much as the loss of his breath. For a moment, he lost track of himself, disoriented. Then a stabbing pain shot up his leg and only the fact that he had lost his breath prevented him from screaming out. Then he was moving backwards, the grip on his ankle drawing him inexorably away.

He looked back and saw that Ranulf's corpse had ahold of his right ankle with its right hand and had dug the claws of its left hand into the meat of the same calf. The corpse wore an expression of insatiable hunger, but beneath that...satisfaction? Glee? Then it pulled with both hands, and any ability to analyze fled Gareth's mind before a second, deeper agony as the claws dug deep furrows in his leg.

Somehow he was screaming. When had he regained his breath? It did not matter. He was caught. He was going to die, and become...

No!

Gareth kicked with his left foot, hard as he could. The sole of his boot impacted the side of Ranulf's head with the snap of breaking bone combined with a sickening squish. The corpse's head canted to the side, knocked off true by the force of Gareth's kick. The tugging on his leg ceased and the pain diminished slightly as the claws' burrowing stopped.

Gareth pushed himself away from the corpse, and his wounded leg slid out of its grasp. Madly, hope surged within him. Had he actually won?

Then the corpse twitched. Again. It moved its hands to its head and, with a quick jerk, set it back aright. Then its gaze leveled on Gareth and its eyes narrowed. He could have sworn he saw fury in that expression.

It pushed itself up onto its hands and knees, then to its feet.

"Bugger me," Gareth said aloud. No, actually he shouted it, he realized as soon as the words left his mouth.

There was no way he could walk, not with his leg wounded as it was. Desperately, he pushed himself away from Ranulf's corpse, scrabbling against the floor tiles with his hands and his left foot. Hatherle! Where was Hatherle!

Grunting and...a curse?...drew Gareth's gaze to the left, and his heart sank. Hatherle was firmly set upon by the other burly corpse. The nimble man servant ducked beneath a raking claw attack, but he bled from cut to his left shoulder and right thigh. He countered then, his longsword whipping toward the corpse's throat, but the things dodged backwards with nearly the agility of a living man. It took a cut to the front of its neck, but seemed to not even notice as it renewed its attack.

They were in trouble.

And then Gareth ran out of time to think. Ranulf's corpse bounded forward and swept its clawed hand down toward him. In desperation, he rolled to the right, bringing his shield up above his body. The corpse's hand struck the shield hard. Harder than any living man could have struck it. Gareth's shoulder flared with pain and he found himself driven into the ground, stunned.

Above him, he heard Ranulf draw back for another attack. Gareth grit his teeth and pushed himself off the floor with his right hand.

He rolled onto his back in time to see the claws sweeping down at him. Somehow, despite the pain in his shoulder, Gareth forced his shield arm up. Again the claws slammed into his shield, and again his arm buckled.

Ranulf pulled his arm back again. Gareth could not take another hit like that; he could barely move his shield arm at all now.

He pushed away, his left heel digging into the crack between two floor stones, but he did not go far enough. He reached out with his right hand, to grab onto to something, anything to pull himself away faster.

His hand came down on a rounded, grainy piece of wood. He blinked and moved his hand up the wood. It was wrapped in leather an inch or so from its end. He knew the feel of that leather like his own flesh.

His axe.

Ranulf's corpse swung at him again. Gareth grabbed the axe and swung it upward with a roar.

Axe met rotting hand in midair, and the axe won. The shock of impact was less than Gareth would have expected; maybe the decay was even more pronounced than it appeared. As a result, his follow-through went farther than he had intended. Had Ranulf pressed the attack, he could have taken Gareth with ease. Instead, the corpse recoiled, an expression that looked almost like pain—or fear? Gareth should be so lucky—flashing across its face.

Ranulf's hand, severed from its arm, landed a few feet away with a dry thud. And began crawling towards Gareth, dragging itself toward him inch by slow inch.

Gareth swallowed hard and kicked himself away from hand and walking corpse alike, fear and revulsion lending his muscles extra strength. He only made it a couple feet before his back hit the wall of the room.

And then he was out of time. The respite ended as Ranulf's corpse charged back in, reaching for Gareth with its good hand and opening its mouth in a snarl, soundless except for the creaking and popping of joints that had long since lost their natural lubrication.

Seated, with his back to the wall, was not a good fighting position, but that was what Gareth had. He was sure not going to end up this thing's lunch, or worse the Necromancer's new pet. He shouted something unintelligible - or at least, *he* had no idea what it was - and shoved himself forward and to the left.

He came down hard on his already injured shoulder and a new surge of pain lanced out. His vision blurred and he saw spots. It was so tempting to just let go and collapse. For half a heartbeat, he almost gave in. Then he felt the breeze of Ranulf's claws passing through the air where his head was a moment before, and he forced himself to his senses.

Gareth looked up to see Ranulf's corpse bent forward next to him, the follow-through from its miss causing it to overbalance slightly, placing all of its weight onto its right knee - the one that just happened to lie within the swinging radius of his axe.

The impact was more substantial when his axe bit into the side of the corpse's knee, but the satisfaction Gareth felt as his blow struck home was even greater. A gravelly crunch advertised the breaking of bones that had been made brittle through desiccation, and the knee gave way, sending Ranulf's corpse sprawling headlong into the wall.

Gareth nearly lost his grip on his axe as the walking corpse fell. The blade caught on something, a piece of bone he thought, for a moment. Panic over being disarmed in such a situation overwhelmed his satisfaction in an eternal instant. Then the bone gave way and the axe pulled free in a small shower of bone fragments and scraps of flesh.

Ranulf's corpse still had its leg, but the knee was ruined, cleaved at least halfway through the bones and connecting tissue, with a large chunk missing where the axe pulled free. It would never again bear Ranulf's weight.

The animated corpse thrashed around when it struck the wall. It tried to lift itself off the floor, but fell again when the stump of its right arm did not perform the way a hand would have. It hesitated, and Gareth imagined he saw something resembling thought in its glowing eyes. Then it placed its good hand on the floor and pulled its legs beneath its body.

The walking corpse pushed itself up onto its feet.

Gareth's jaw dropped open and he felt his eyes growing wide as his bowels turned to water with fear. No! It could not do that!

But it had. It righted itself and turned its head to regard Gareth coldly, without feeling or though. Except, perhaps...was that grudging respect in its unearthly gaze?

Gareth scrambled backwards, but the blood from his wounded leg made the stones of the floor slick and he got no traction. His terror increased. He was going to die! Die, and become a slave in undeath.

The corpse opened its jaw in a macabre imitation of a smile, and it stepped toward Gareth.

The knee gave way completely.

Gareth reacted out of pure instinct. He rolled onto his right side, putting his shield between himself and Ranulf's corpse as it fell atop him. The weight of the impact was substantial, but less than he would have expected had Ranulf been alive. Still, he found himself driven onto his back, his shield arm splayed out uselessly to his side.

Ranulf clawed at him. Gareth grit his teeth in anticipation of further agony, and was surprised when it did not come. Instead, the corpse's claws simply scraped harmlessly down the front of his breastplate with a sickening high-pitched squeak.

The thing must truly have been without thought. How else could it have made such a mistake? Beside himself with a mixture of relief and incredulity, Gareth remained still while the claws completed their transit of his armor. The horrid blue lights in Ranulf's eyes flared with chagrin, or confusion, or...

Gareth did not stop to consider what exactly what was or was not going through the thing's head.

Silently blessing the fates that led it to blunder at that exact moment, he raised his axe even as the corpse drew back its own hand for another attack, then plunged it down toward Ranulf's head.

The sound Gareth's axe made as it clove through the side of his old drinking companion's head was solid, final. Sickening. In spite of himself, he felt a tinge of regret, guilt almost, as the gruesome light in the corpse's eyes flickered and went out.

5

Hatherle tied off the final stitch in Gareth's calf with a particularly rough jerk. It hurt. Not as much as what Hatherle did with his shoulder, but it hurt. Gareth grimaced and had to suppress a snide comment; it would not do to upset Hatherle after he had gone to all the trouble of playing doctor.

Besides, the man servant had emerged from the battle with the animated corpses quite a lot better off than Gareth had. That was worth quite a bit.

"Thanks, Hatherle," Gareth said after he regained his breath.

"Of course, my lord," Hatherle replied. He took a moment to coil the remaining thread then he tucked it and the needle he was using into a case, which he placed inside his pack. Then he stood and offered Gareth a hand.

It took some doing, since he outweighed Hatherle by a fair amount, even without the heavy steel of his breastplate, bracers, and greaves. But after a bit of huffing and puffing Gareth got to his feet. The pain in his right calf immediately flared, growing worse from the weight suddenly placed upon it.

"Son of a whore," Gareth muttered, earning a quirked eyebrow from Hatherle.

"It will be some weeks before you regain full use of the leg, my lord," he said in a clinical tone that Gareth had come to recognize well. "For that matter, your shoulder will be some time in recovery as well. Just because I was able to force it back into its joint does not mean..."

"Got it, Hatherle. Anything else?"

The serving man shook his head, and Gareth felt a small surge of relief. He was right, of course.

Hatherle was always right. That was why he did such great business as a scholar-for-hire - Hatherle preferred the term Sage, but what was the difference? - before the incident with the bandits that led him to swearing fealty to Gareth. It would have been nice if he were wrong this time, though. Since Hatherle had worked his magic, Gareth's shoulder almost felt good again. Sore, but at least he could move it. He would not want to test that under combat conditions, though. Or his leg, for what it was worth.

And here they were, within the Necromancer's domain. Small chance he would just let them go so they could come back when Gareth was fully healed and ready. He nodded, resigned.

"I just hope the stitches hold. There will be more action ahead."

Hatherle's other eyebrow joined its twin, high on his forehead. "My Lord?" He cleared his throat, taking a moment to glance back at the shattered cell and the now unmoving corpses littering the room. "Perhaps it would be more prudent to go."

Gareth had to suppress an amused smile. For once, he had made the leap of logic before his man servant? Wonders never ceased, it seemed.

"If I thought we had a chance of making it out without conflict, we would be on our way now," he said, truthfully. "That Necromancer will not let us escape, though. And besides," he gestured toward the ceiling they had apparently fallen through - somewhat more believable with the new hole in it, he had to admit, "we cannot go the way we came. Do you have any idea where the exit is from here?"

Hatherle shook his head and his lips lowered into a frown. Was that uncertainty Gareth saw in his eyes?

"Don't worry, Hatherle. We'll be fine. You'll see." Gareth heard the undertones in his voice as he spoke, and was surprised to not hear the mountain of uncertainty he felt come through. Maybe he was getting better at this 'being a leader' bit. Hatherle was not the first who seemed to expect it of him, though he was the first to flat out swear himself to Gareth's service. Crazy fellow.

Hatherle just looked at him in silence. Gareth began to grow somewhat uncomfortable under his gaze.

Finally, Hatherle grunted and said, "Very well, my lord." He stepped back toward the cell and bent over. When he returned, he held a length of metal out toward Gareth: the upper half from one of the broken bars. "Makeshift, but this should work as a crutch."

Gareth blinked. A crutch? What did he... He moved slightly, settling more weight upon his injured leg, and almost collapsed from the immediate protest his wounds made.

Indeed. A crutch was quite the thing.

He made a shallow nod of thanks then took the length of metal. It was bent and, where it had been sheared off under the force of the animated corpse's prybar, jagged. But it was about the right length. So he placed the jagged end on the ground, the more gently rounded end under his arm, and tried to take a step.

It hurt.

But it worked. He was at least slightly mobile again. That was the best he could hope for.

42

❧ 6 ❧

There was not much to the level of the tower - assuming they really were within the Necromancer's tower and not somewhere else - that held the room with their cell. The doorway opened into a featureless hallway that encircled the room completely. And did not appear to have any other exits. It was well-lit, but there was no obvious source of the light. It was just...there. It was more than a bit unsettling.

They made two complete circuits of the hallway before Gareth finally stopped. This was getting nowhere, and besides his leg hurt like hell. He needed a rest.

"Now what?"

"It defies probability that there is no way to get to and from this level," Hatherle said, his voice contemplative.

Gareth snorted. "He's a bloody spellcaster. For all we know he could just...you know..." he waved his left hand in the air "...poof himself to and fro."

Hatherle shook his head. "I've heard that sort of spell is very difficult and requires great skill. But more importantly, it is very expensive."

Gareth looked askance at him. "Come again?"

"The components required for a spell like that are very rare, or so the writings say."

"You would know, oh sage of sages." Gareth sighed and straightened his back. It had felt good to slouch, to put more weight on the makeshift crutch. Alas, there was work to be done still if he wanted to see his own bed again.

Hatherle inclined his head in response to Gareth's words, a flash of a smile appearing on his face for a moment. He had apparently decided to take the remark as a compliment. Good thing, too, because Gareth had not meant it as an insult. A friendly jibe, a bit of teasing maybe, but certainly not an insult.

"Alright. Let's makes another pass." He forced the little voice, now grown quite a bit larger after the first two laps, in his head that begged him to quit and sit down into the back of his head. This was no time for ninnies. "Check the floor and walls carefully as we go."

As we go more slowly, he meant. There was no need for him to even considering voicing the thought, however. Hatherle lagged considerably during the lap, forcing Gareth to slow his pace to avoid leaving him behind.

The man was an absolute saint sometimes.

They had almost completed a third circuit before Hatherle found it.

It should have been Gareth. It was on his side of the corridor. But the ever increasing protests from his injured calf had begun intruding ever more steadily onto his consciousness until it was all he could do to put one foot in front of the next without breaking down. And to blazes with the makeshift crutch. It had helped a first. Hell, it still helped. But the blunt end was beginning to dig into his armpit something fierce, becoming almost as much a source of discomfort as assistance.

All that was lost when Hatherle spoke up, though. Well, most of it.

Gareth bit back a curse as he turned to look at the spot in the wall where Hatherle was pointing, and had to admit the revelation hardly suppressed any of his discomfort at all. But at least it provided a distraction.

At first he could not see it. Hatherle was crouched next to the wall, pointing eagerly at a place just an inch above the floor. But there was nothing to see to Gareth's eyes. He was just about to tell Hatherle to stop being a bloody fool when he recalled the carvings in the alcove.

He moved backwards, away from Hatherle and whatever he was looking at. Still nothing. Gareth moved again, and struck the opposite wall. Nothing. That left just one more thing. He gritted his teeth in anticipation of pain to come and bent his legs, lowering himself into a deep a crouch as he could manage without either passing out from pain or falling over.

And then he saw it.

It was the same symbol as was on the ceiling of the alcove in the cave, carved into the stove as though by a fine chisel. But it did not come into view until he had lowered his line of sight. Which meant it was not a simple carving at all, but some sort of magical sigil. Just like in the alcove.

Gareth grinned. "Well done, Hatherle," he said. He straightened his legs and very nearly fell down; if he had not had the piece of metal there was no way he would not have. All the same, he had to take a deep breath and forced the protests from his injured leg away before he could speak again. "What now?"

Hatherle's triumphant smile faded slightly and he shrugged. "I doubt it functions the same as the sigil in the cave, my lord. Could be this is just a lure to draw us in..."

"A lure leading nowhere?"

Hatherle inclined his head, conceding the point. "In which case it likely marks the location of something important."

Thanks for stating the obvious, Gareth did not say. "Well, play with it. See if you can get it do do something."

Hatherle nodded and turned to the sigil. He began probing it with his fingers, and Gareth winced. That was probably not a good idea. *He* really should be the one to do this... Stupid leg.

Gareth watched his man servant working on the sigil, impatience born from frustration and embarrassment at his own ineffectiveness growing all the while. Finally he could not contain it any more.

"Anything?"

A slight shrug accompanied Hatherle's response. "There appears to be a small protrusion here, near the wolf's snout. Maybe if I press it..."

Hatherle's hand moved and there was a loud CLICK that echoed down the hallway.

This was either going to be very good or very bad. Gareth would not give odds either way.

Gareth found himself counting the seconds in his head as nothing else happened. At ten, though, he began to hear a low rumbling from beneath the floor. It grew louder over the next several seconds and the floor began to shake slightly. Then, at thirty, the paving stones in the floor before he and Hatherle began to rise up. At the same time, the stone ceiling began to pull back, creating an opening above. Finally, the stones' movement stopped and there was a stone staircase leading upward where before there was only the circling hallway.

The two men stepped back. Hatherle looked stunned; Gareth had no doubt he looked similarly.

"Well." Gareth cleared his throat. "That did the trick."

"Indeed, my Lord."

"I guess this confirms that we *are* in the Necromancer's tower. Seems we have to up to get down."

Gareth looked up the stairs, then down at his injured leg. This was not going to be easy. But there was no point dilly-dallying. He took a deep breath and hauled himself up the first step.

"Let's go."

❧ 7 ❧

The stairs climbed for what seemed forever, circling in the same manner as the hallway below. After ten steps, Gareth's injured leg was screaming in protest and he had to sit down to rest before continuing. Hatherle kept a watch, his longsword at the ready, as Gareth worked out the kinks as best he could. But it took far too long to get moving again. The Necromancer had to know of their movements - this was his tower, after all - and he was doubtless preparing the next surprise for them. Gareth half expected to hear footsteps descending toward them at any moment. But that did not happen, and after a few minutes he felt ready to continue upwards.

Ten more stairs and Gareth was sorely tempted to sit again. But he instead gritted his teeth and pushed on. No need to give the Necromancer any more time than necessary.

Finally, the staircase ended at a small landing that backed up to a stout wooden door that was reinforced with strips of iron. It was ordained only with an iron ring where a doorknob would be and a dark iron square in the center of the door, about at eye level, which was engraved with Necromancer's wolf and deer sigil.

Gareth paused on the landing and looked the door over. Nothing seemed unusual about it, but he had a feeling there was more there than met the eye. Not that anything so far had met with expectations, so why should this door?

"I wonder what sort of trap the Necromancer may have placed here?" Hatherle said, echoing Gareth's thoughts.

"Not sure. Why don't you try it, and we'll see?"

Gareth glanced aside at Hatherle, a teasing smile forming on his lips, in time to see the serving man flinch then square his shoulders and take a deep breath. He stepped forward toward the door.

"No!" Gareth said, forcefully. "Goodness, man, I was joking."

Hatherle blinked, then frowned back at Gareth, his expression one of reproach.

Gareth rolled his eyes. One of these days he was going to figure out the fellow's sense of humor. Some day.

"Hit it with a piece of wood or something first. Do you have any more torches?"

Hatherle nodded and pulled his pack off. He rummaged through it for a moment then put it back on, unlit torch in hand. "Brace yourself, my lord," he said, then he reached out and tapped the door with the torch.

Nothing happened.

The two men exchanged glances, Hatherle's questioning. Gareth shrugged and waved him onward.

Hatherle tapped the door again, this time on one of the iron strips. Again nothing. The same with the iron ring and square. He shrugged again and set the torch down, then reached out and took hold of the ring with his bare hand.

Hatherle stiffened and let out a low groan. His body began shaking.

"Hatherle!" Gareth surged forward, ignoring a stab of pain from his leg, and pulled the man servant back. His grip loosened from the door easily and very quickly he was back out of danger.

"Are you alright?" Concerned, Gareth looked him over. Only to find him wearing...an impish grin.

"Pardon, my lord," Hatherle said. "Just joking."

Dumbfounded, Gareth stared at him in shock for a long moment. Sudden anger conflicted with relief and then finally gave way to wry amusement, and he found himself laughing, his earlier thought about Hatherle's sense of humor returning to mind, ironically.

"Bloody hell, man, don't do that again," he said. He could not force his tone to sternness, however much he wanted to.

Hatherle's smile slipped a bit, and he nodded. "At any rate," he said after clearing his throat softly, "the ring does not appear to have any function, my lord. It did not rotate, and would not budge when I pulled on it."

Gareth frowned and looked back at the door. His eyes alighted on the iron square, and the Necromancer's sigil. "That must be the key," he murmured, and stepped forward to examine it more closely.

The sigil was the same as it had been the last two times, the square of iron plain, unadorned. The sigil was engraved in the iron, but not deeply; Gareth ran his hand over the square and could barely feel the lines of the engraving. He could not see or feel any part of it that stood out in any way. Yet it must be there. The previous sigils had pointed the way; this one must as well.

Unless this was all a sick joke of some kind, designed to keep them running around pointlessly until the Necromancer was ready to take them out. Or until they died of thirst or hunger.

That thought made Gareth's stomach growl; they had eaten through what small morsels they brought with them during their stay in the cage, and the water flasks were running low as well. The Necromancer, if he had been keeping tabs on them - and Gareth was certain that was the case, had to know or suspect their state of affairs. And why go to the trouble of killing them when he could just let nature take care of it for him?

The was a depressing thought.

"Is it just me, my lord," Hatherle said, from behind Gareth's shoulder, "or are the wolf's and deer's eyes a bit larger on this sigil?"

Gareth did a double-take and peered at the sigil more closely. "I'm not sure. I suppose maybe. What if I..." He reached out and touched his fingertips to the eyes of both beasts.

There was another resonating CLICK, this time from within the door itself.

Gareth retreated, as much a retreat as he could manage with his leg anyway. After several seconds, nothing more happened and he let out the breath he was holding. If they were lucky, the click was the door's locking mechanism acting in response to his touching the sigil that way. He did not want to think about what it could be if they were unlucky.

Gareth took a few moments to shift his axe into his left hand. It would be of no use trying to wield it in his right, not with the crutch he needed to use. Then he had Hatherle strap the shield onto his right upper arm. It was an awkward fit, but at least it would offer some small amount of protection.

Hatherle prepared himself, drawing steel and getting good grip on his sword. Then, at a nod from Gareth, he grabbed the ring on the door and pulled.

❧ 8 ☙

The door swung open immediately, revealing...a plush office.

Plush was probably not the right word to use to describe the room beyond the door, but it was the only one that sprung to Gareth's mind. The room was circular, about the same size as the cell room on the level below. And probably located directly above it. It was well lit by a number of gilded stand lamps, though the lamps were not burning any sort of visible fuel, leaving the question of what was producing the light unanswered. The floor was stone, but covered in thick red rugs that were lined in thread-of-gold tassels. A trio of full bookshelves were spaced equidistantly around the perimeter, and there was another wood and iron door directly across from the entrance. In the center, facing the open door, was a long desk that was constructed out of dark reddish wood and polished until it gleamed. A quill and ink lay to one side, opposite a stack of papers, but aside from that the desk was clear. A pair of chairs, simple but of obvious high quality, and padded, were arranged before the desk, to receive visitors no doubt.

The Necromancer sat at the desk. He was garbed

as before and appeared completely at ease as he regarded Gareth and Hatherle over steepled fingers.

Gareth stood rooted to the spot for a moment in surprise. Of all the ways he thought to meet the Necromancer again, *this* was not one of them.

The moment stretched, then the Necromancer broke the silence by slowly clapping his hands together.

"Well done, gentlemen. I am impressed." He gestured toward the empty chairs. "Will you sit? I'm certain your leg must be paining you by now."

Gareth, taken aback, remained silent as he hobbled into the room. After all that had happened, *this* was all the Necromancer had to say? Amazing. And even more amazing, he looked as though he was genuinely concerned about Gareth's comfort. Gareth made a mental note to use this man as a comparison for any actors he ever watched perform in the future. He was good.

"I prefer to stand," he said in reply.

The Necromancer shrugged. "As you wish. May I offer you and your man some wine, to take the edge off?"

"Thank you, no." Gareth spoke quickly, seeing Hatherle licking his lips with poorly-suppressed eagerness. He had seen the former sage in a wine bottle enough to recognize that weakness and nip it in the bud quickly.

Again the Necromancer shrugged. He took a moment to pull open one of the drawers in his desk and remove a wine bottle and a simple but obviously well-made goblet. He poured the wine, and the faintest hint of its aroma wafted across to Gareth's nose. Oh my. To smell that good from that far away - it must have been a heavenly vintage. His thirst, growing all the more intense by the second especially now that he could see drinkable fluid so close by, screamed at him to just have a drink. What could it hurt? It took a force of will to not renege on his refusal, but he managed. Somehow.

The Necromancer smelled the wine with closed eyes and a serene smile on his lips, then lifted the goblet to his lips and sipped. Enjoyment seemed to flow through him. When he opened his eyes, they twinkled with an inner light they did not have before.

"I fear we've gotten off on the wrong foot," the Necromancer said.

Gareth snorted. "Says the man who locked us in a cage and then ordered my friend's corpse to kill us. Can't see how that could have gone right."

The Necromancer raised one eyebrow as he fixed Gareth with a contemptuous gaze. "You broke into my house with the intent to kill me. How would *you* respond to that, hmm?"

His words sunk in and Gareth had to admit he had a valid point. Still...it's not like the Necromancer was some peace-loving fellow who just sat around minding his own business all day. He was, well, a Necromancer. Those sorts of people were just a menace.

He was clearly waiting for Gareth to respond. Gareth obliged him with a noncommittal shrug, but said nothing. There was not much to say, and besides, his leg was beginning to ache...bad. Gareth was half afraid if he spoke too much, his discomfort would show through. And though the Necromancer knew he was probably in some measure of discomfort, it would not do for Gareth to give him a more accurate estimate of his condition.

After a short moment of silence, the Necromancer, too shrugged. "No matter, I suppose." He took another sip from his goblet. "What do you hope to accomplish here?"

Gareth was taken aback. This was not going *at all*

the way he had envisioned. Attacking monsters, parrying blows, taking down foes - those things he could deal with, and expected on a job like this. Reasoned discourse? That was another matter altogether.

"Just looking to collect a bounty," he said, in as straightforward a tone as he could manage.

The Necromancer smirked. "It's all about the money, isn't it." Sipping his wine again, he looked amused more than anything else. "So you have no interest in rooting out my *evil*," his voice dripped sarcasm as he said that, "or of righting whatever wrongs I have committed?"

"Well, there *is* that, too, now that you get to it."

The Necromancer was silent for a moment, then burst out laughing. It sounded genuine and was disturbingly human, not at all the maniacal laugh one would expect from the depraved and evil. "Ah, my friend," he said after his laughter subsided, "you are droll. Which is something I can very much appreciate, I assure you."

Gareth did not respond. Beside him, Hatherle shifted on his feet, his expression one of distaste.

The Necromancer noted this, and the amusement faded from his features. "Your man does not approve of me. But then, he is clearly not as...practical...as you."

Gareth could almost hear Hatherle's teeth grinding, and for a moment he thought he would have to restrain the former sage from doing something rash. But in the end, Hatherle restrained himself, even schooling his expression to one of stoic readiness. Though knowing him as he did, Gareth could tell he was more than a little peeved.

"What would you say if I were to tell you I understand your friend's disapproval. And your Lord's as well."

"I bow to no Lord."

The Necromancer snorted. "Tell yourself that if you wish, but we both know the truth." He set the goblet down on his desk and leaned forward. He clasped his hands together and regarded Gareth with an earnest expression. "If I were in their shoes, or yours for that matter, I expect I would disapprove of me as well." His eyes narrowed, his stare becoming severe, piercing. "But they do not know the facts. If they did, they would sing my praises, not set trifling bounties on my head."

Gareth snorted again. Five hundred crowns was far from trifling. With that much money, he could buy himself some property, settle down, give up the life of a wandering sellsword. Sellaxe. Whatever. Not that he would. He knew himself well enough to admit he enjoyed the work. Most times. But still, it would be possible.

"You don't believe me?"

Gareth blinked in confusion. It took a second to realize the Necromancer misunderstood his snort. Although truth be told, now that he considered it, he truly did not believe the various priests and Lords, let alone the rest of the people out there, would change their views on Necromancy any time soon. "Can't say I do," he said, honestly.

"What if I told you that all this," the Necromancer waved his hand, including the entire room, the entire tower, in his statement, "existed for one purpose only." His eyes flashed with something. Passion? Reverence? Insanity? "I believe I am close to discovering a way to defeat death."

"Beg pardon?"

"Death is the price all men pay, my friend. But does it have to be? What if there were a way to eliminate death completely?" The Necromancer's pace of speech increased, his tone becoming more impassioned, excited. "How much suffering, how many crimes, have their root in a fear of death? How much better could humanity be if that weight were lifted from its shoulders?" He grinned. It was an unnatural-looking smile, the upward curving of his lips revealing his gleaming white teeth and making him looking almost like a carnival freak. "I am almost there. I only need a short time more and I will have it, the answer to every man's desire."

Gareth had to work to suppress a shudder. The man *was* insane. He had to be. Right off the top of his head, Gareth could think of half a dozen terrible consequences of a discovery like that, if it was even possible. Which he seriously doubted.

"So what, you want me to go back and tell Lord Hadley to just leave you alone? I don't think he will buy that."

The Necromancer's smile faded, becoming instead a frown of annoyance. "I have no faith in his ability to reason. Though you *could* assist me in another way."

Here it was. Gareth flexed his fingers on the grip of his axe, willing his muscles to relax into readiness. "And how is that, exactly?"

"You are clearly very capable. None have made it as far into my realm as you, or defeated as many of my servants. I could use a man like you at my side, watching my back, managing my forces."

He was joking, right? Gareth opened his mouth to retort, but the Necromancer beat him to it.

"Unfortunately," said the Necromancer with a malicious grin that was, if possible, even worse than his earlier one, "you are no use to me alive."

He made a little flick of his left hand, and Gareth heard a sharp CLICK from behind him. He turned to see that the doorway he had entered through had changed. Before it opened onto a landing; now it led into a large room that was empty except for a number of columns running down its length.

And a horde of animated corpses.

$\maltese$ 9 $\maltese$

Gareth should not have been surprised. What else could he expect from a man such as the Necromancer? All the same, he could not deny that the man's genteel demeanor had lulled him into lowering his guard. So when the first pair of corpses stormed through the door and reached toward him and Hatherle, Gareth stood rooted to the spot in shock.

"Goodbye, my friends," the Necormancer said from behind. "If it comforts you at all, I am very confident your passing will help me make great progress toward the goal." Did he really expect Gareth to find that notion appealing? "Who knows, you may end up being the key to the entire experiment."

Another click from behind. Gareth looked back quickly, in time to see the latch on the door on the other side of the room lowering into place. The Necromancer was gone.

Then the corpse was on him. Dead fingers clawed through the air toward his face. Reflexes honed through years of training saved him on the first pass as he turned his body away, placing his right shoulder - and the shield strapped to his arm - closest to his attacker. The claws struck the shield and scraped harmlessly down it, though the sound they caused as they did so made his hair stand on end.

There was no time for subtlety. He lunged forward, ignoring the screams of protest from his injured calf, and brought his axe straight down atop the corpse's head. It split open like a melon and the corpse instantly stopped, falling to the floor at Gareth's feet in a heap and spilling grey matter—it was surprisingly fluid, and rank; the poor fellow must not have died the first time all that long ago—all over the floor.

Beside him, Hatherle was hard pressed. His wounds were not as bad as Gareth's had been, but he did not have the advantage of Gareth's years of training. What he knew of the sword, and combat, was what Gareth and his various acquaintances had taught him. This corpse was more nimble than the last couple Hatherle had faced, easily dodging a riposte from the slender man and responding with a bullrush attack that knocked him to the floor.

Hatherle's expression when Gareth's axe took the corpse's head form its shoulders was a classic blend of relief and revulsion. And small wonder; Gareth would not have enjoyed being splattered with corpse-fluids either.

Gareth helped Hatherle to his feet as best he could, but was drawn up short by the renewed pain in his leg. He glanced down and saw that his pants bore fresh bloodstains. He could feel fluid seeping into his boot; one or more of his stitches must have pulled. Damnit.

"Thankee, my lord," Hatherle began, but then there was no more time for talk as another pair of corpses entered the room.

Those were more easily dispatched. The men were

not surprised this time, and both corpses were older, more brittle and less quick.

Still, it was obvious, from the multitude still approaching the door, that they would be overwhelmed sooner or later.

Another pair of corpses shouldered their way through the door and Gareth lurched forward to intercept them.

"Hatherle, the door!"

Hatherle nodded and ducked to the side. The corpse nearest him turned to follow, but Gareth leapt to place himself ahead of the monster.

Or rather, he tried to. His right leg, already pressed beyond what would have been prudent, picked that moment to fail him completely. Gareth fell hard, taking a painful bump on his cheek as his face struck the floor. Above the pain, he felt a surge of despair. He missed his chance, and the animated corpse was going to get to Hatherle before he could get the door shut. They were going to be overwhelmed, overrun.

Then something struck him in the side and an instant later he felt a weight land on his back. Whatever it was thrashed around, and it stank of decay. The corpse! It must have tripped over him and fallen.

Hardly believing his luck, Gareth squirmed and pushed with all his might, trying to get out from beneath the undead thing before it realized what it had fallen upon and choked the life out of him. Fortunately, being reanimated did not seem to convey intellect very well - at least with this corpse; Gareth tried not to think about how quick Ranulf had seemed - and Gareth managed to get some distance from the thing with just a very little struggle.

He pushed himself to his knees to find the corpse also rising. His axe ended that, severing the thing's desiccated left leg at the knee. It flopped onto the floor; Gareth would have sworn it was surprised by that turn of events, if he was not sure it had no mind to be surprised with. Its surprise, if it existed, was momentary, though, before Gareth's axe split its head in two.

Gareth was just beginning to feel good about himself and their chances when something grabbed him by the back of his breastplate, lifted him off his knees, and threw him into one of the bookshelves.

The impact was incredible. He struck it with his already-injured shoulder, sending a surge of pain through him that was so intense he could only see red for what felt like eternity. He did not feel himself strike the floor, or anything at all for that matter, except for the pain.

Somewhere in his mind a voice screamed at him to get up, to move, to do something, because if he did not, he was dead. But that voice was faint, easily ignored beneath the screaming agony that washed over him. Had the end come right then, he would have welcomed it without hesitation.

But somehow, it did not.

Some time later, he had no idea how long, his vision cleared and the pain faded so that he could process other things. At first, all he could see was a blur, but after blinking a few times, he was able to make out a face staring down at him.

Hatherle's face.

The man servant looked like hell. He had a deep cut running across his forehead and down the right side of his face toward his ear. It had bled intensely, coating his face with a sheen of red that at first made Gareth think he was a devil of some sort. But devil's never wore expressions of concern that melted away into joyous smiles when the object of their attention awoke. Or whatever the right term was for what Gareth did when he came back to his senses.

"Are you well, my lord?"

Gareth barked out a bitter laugh. Or at least he hoped it was a laugh; it was hard to tell. "Do I look well?"

Hatherle shook his head and helped Gareth to his feet. As he stood up - he very nearly collapsed again when his wounded leg felt even a small amount of weight - he looked around.

The door to the room full of animated corpses was shut, but it shuddered periodically as something, no several somethings, pounded on it from the other side. The corpse Gareth had done for lay where he expected it. The other, the one that had thrown him across the room, was slumped against the desk. The blade of Hatherle's sword was stuck into its eye and protruded through the back of its skull. Only the blade.

Gareth blinked. Hatherle was not strong enough to make that strong a thrust. "What happened?"

Hatherle shrugged. "I got the door shut as it," he nodded toward the impaled corpse, "threw you. I tried to distract it, but it was so strong." The slender man paused, swallowing. "It leapt on me, and impaled itself on my sword somehow. But it did not stop immediately. I tried to pull the sword out, but..." He gestured toward the ground near the desk, where the pommel of his sword lay. The blade was sheared off near the crosspiece.

Cold anger burned inside Gareth as he considered everything that had happened to them over the last hours, or was it days? "Let's go, Hatherle. I'm going to kill that bastard."

Hatherle nodded agreement. "Let me check your leg first, my lord."

Gareth hated to take the time, but the shuddering door seemed solid enough, at least for the time being. But Hatherle was right. He had burst at least one stitch, and he would not be able to fight well if he was losing blood.

A few minutes later, Gareth shouldered his way through the door the Necromancer had disappeared through, ready to deal out some punishment.

❧ 10 ❧

Gareth did not truly expect to find the Necromancer on the other side of the door. More likely it would lead to another corridor with confusing twists and turns and more riddles to solve. Or even better, to some sort of magical trap that would burn he and Hatherle alive while the Necromancer watched and laughed.

So when he forced his way through the portal and found himself in a well-appointed bed chamber, and the Necromancer bent over a small chest of drawers next to the four-poster bed that dominated the room, he found himself stopping in complete surprise.

Which meant he was at best half as surprised as the Necromancer, from the look on the skinny man's face.

"What?" said the Necromancer. "How?" His eyes flickered from Gareth to the door to Hatherle and back to the door.

"Were you expecting someone else?" asked Gareth as he stalked, limped really, and calling it limping was being charitable, toward him. He swung his axe slowly back and forth at his side, and he knew he had a murderous expression on his face, an expression he had practiced long and hard, one that had struck fear into strong men on many occasions before this.

The Necromancer was not a strong man, at least not physically. But, credit where credit's due, if he felt fear he never let it surface. "Actually yes."

"Sorry to disappoint." Gareth reached the corner of the bed and rounded it, grabbing the corner post with his right hand to steady himself as he did so. The Necromancer was almost within reach. Gareth should have known better.

The Necromancer smirked slightly, then inclined his head toward Gareth. "I did not think you would be able to fight my servants off, given their numbers. Not in your condition."

"And they say wizards are smart." Gareth did not even try to keep the scorn, the derision, from his tone. No point in showing respect to a man whose brains you were about to splatter all over his fine rug.

"Oh, we are."

The Necromancer snapped his fingers, and everything went black.

He was not dead.

That was a surprise, actually. Gareth had heard wizards could kill easily with their magic. Presumably, Necromancers, as attuned to death as they were, would be particularly adept at it. But when several seconds passed and he found he could hear his heart pounding in his ears, smell the faint odor of the freshly re-killed corpses in the adjoining room, feel the sweat beading his brow, Gareth was certain he still lived.

But for how long?

He realized he had dropped into a combat crouch, his reflexes responding to the changing condition even as his mind struggled to make sense of it. His injured leg screamed at him; the crouch was pulling on his stitches again. He could feel them, about to give way. But he pushed away the impulse to straighten, instead forcing himself to move forward, toward where he last saw the Necromancer.

Something passed over his head, causing a slight breeze that ruffled his hair.

Behind him, he heard a surprised-sounding grunt, then a long slow sigh followed by a limp thump. That could only have been Hatherle hitting the floor.

Gareth clenched his teeth in anger and turned toward the sound, raising his axe in preparation for a swing. He may not be able to see the Necromancer, but he could damn well hear him. He was not going to get away without tasting the bite of Gareth's axe!

Or at least that was the plan.

Suddenly something snatched the axe out of his hand. One moment he was holding it in readiness: not in a death grip, but hardly loosely by any means. The next, the axe was gone, plucked from his hand before he could even think to resist, and with a strength that would have been irresistible regardless.

Gareth had only a heartbeat to wonder what had happen before he felt a vice take hold of his throat and lift him off his feet.

Shock, pain, and sudden loss of breath all worked in unison to confuse him; it took longer than it should have to realize that the vice was in fact a hand. Thin, skeletal fingers wrapped around his throat with a strength Gareth never imagined possible. Panicked horror surged through him. It was another of those walking corpses!

Then a voice spoke in the darkness, its source mere inches in front of his face from the stirring of the air. "You fool," it said in a tone that dripped contempt. "You actually thought you could defeat me." A half-laugh, half-snort punctuated the words. "Now it is you who are defeated, and I gain a new pair of servants."

The Necromancer. It was the Necromancer speaking, and who had hold of Gareth's throat. Why had it taken so long to recognize his voice?

Gareth's heart pounded all the louder. He began seeing flashes of light in the darkness and his lungs cried out as though ready to burst. He had to get out of the Necromancer's grip. Had to breathe.

But flailing with his hand was like beating on a

tree trunk, for all the result it had in getting the man to remove his hand from around Gareth's throat. Amazing that so scrawny a fellow could harbor such strength!

The Necromancer laughed again, in amusement. Gareth imagined he could see, somewhere behind the flashes of light, the other man's lips turned upward into a mocking sneer. It was not an image he wanted as his last.

He tried to struggle more, to strike the Necromancer with the edge of his shield, but his right arm would not move; it was too heavy. Hell, his *free* arm felt like it was made of lead.

He could definitely see the Necromancer now. Whatever he had done to get rid of the light had faded. Or then again, maybe not. The edges of Gareth's vision contained only darkness, which was slowly spreading toward the center. After a moment, he realized when the darkness spread fully, it would be all over, and felt another surge of fear. That fear turned to terror when the thought passed ever so slowly through his head that it might not be all over. Would he be aware of himself, of his status, once the Necromancer turned him into one of his undead servants?

He had to escape. He raised his arm, leaden as it was, to punch the Necromancer in the face. But the blow fell well short of its mark and his hand dropped, limply, down until his hand fell onto something on Gareth's belt.

The Necromancer's sneer grew more gleeful. "Soon, my friend," he said in a tone that was nearly a purr.

The growing darkness had eclipsed the room, its furniture, Hatherle lying face-down on the floor, everything except for the Necromancer's face.

It could not end like this. Gareth tried to clench his

fist for one last attack, but for some reason his fist would not close. Something prevented his fingers from reaching his palm. Something round, hard. Something cold.

The pommel of his dagger, where it was sheathed on his belt.

Final desperation gave strength to his fingers as Gareth clutched at the dagger's grip and withdrew it from its sheath.

The Necromancer's eyes flickered downward as he noticed Gareth's movement. They went wide, the sneer leaving his face to be replaced by an expression of shocked disbelief as Gareth plunged the blade into his chest.

He was definitely dead this time. He had to be; all he saw was darkness, all he felt was cold.

But then, once again, the light slowly returned, revealing the bed chamber's ceiling, Gareth had to consider that maybe his assumption had been wrong on that point. He blinked, focusing in on a hand that was reaching down toward him, then followed the hand up to its owner.

Hatherle was crouched by his side. He still had that nasty bloody gash across his forehead, but now the other half of his face was bruising up as well. Somehow the un-bruised half of his face was ashen beneath all the blood, as though he was deathly afraid. Small wonder, that. Despite all that, however, he somehow managed to look ready for action.

A lot better than Gareth felt.

Gareth took Hatherle's hand, and the man servant pulled him to his feet. There he had to stand still for a long moment, leaning against the former sage for support to avoid falling again as the world spun around him. Finally it settled down and he examined his surroundings.

The bed chamber looked the same as it had, but

the Necromancer was nowhere to be seen. Blood stained the stone floor where he had been - or where Gareth thought he had been - but that was all.

"What happened?" he asked.

Hatherle shrugged. "When I came to, you were unconscious, my Lord, and our foe had vanished." He held up his free hand; he was carrying Gareth's blood-stained dagger. "This was lying on the floor."

Gareth nodded and took back the dagger, cleaning it on his pants leg before re-sheathing it. "He hit you on the head."

It was not a question, but Hatherle nodded any-way. "In the darkness, my Lord. I heard him coming, but he was too fast, and..." He left off talking, sounding embarrassed.

Gareth snorted. "He got the better of both of us, Hatherle. Don't beat yourself up." He took a hesitant step toward the pool of blood. When he did not im-mediately fall over, he took another, then crouched down next to it, again ignoring the protest from his leg. "I can't imagine he would have not killed us with magic. Why didn't he? Why fisticuffs?" he said aloud, glancing over his shoulder toward Hatherle.

Hatherle shook his head. "I concur, my lord." He swallowed. Hard. The color was slowly beginning to return to the unbruised portion of his face. "Of course, killing magic takes some preparation. Likely he had not planned on using those sort of spells when he set out his plan for the day. Or he just figured his minions would do the job well enough."

"Or he really *does* like me."

Hatherle looked at him askance. "I suppose that is...possible."

So where did he go? There was only one other exit besides the one leading to the office, an iron-rein-forced door that swung open easily at Gareth's touch. Beyond the door were stairs leading straight downward until it reached a landing some thirty feet below. Unlike the previous corridors, however, this stairwell was illuminated by natural sunlight that streamed in through periodic windows on the left wall and through a stained glass design inlaid above the door down on the landing.

"That can't be the exit...can it?" It was too easy.

Hatherle made no reply, but the hopeful expression on his face said it all.

Gareth sighed. The Necromancer was gone and, frankly, Gareth had no desire to figure out where he had gone to. For whatever reason, it looked as though there would be no payoff on this one. Lord Hadley had been quite clear on that point: no body, no bounty.

A great thump, much louder than any of the previous, reverberated into the bed chamber from the office. Hatherle looked back, and blanched.

"The door is almost off its hinges. I'm not sure what hit it, but..." He left the rest unsaid.

"Let's get out of here." Gareth hated to leave with nothing to show for this expedition, but that was how it was. He turned back toward the stairway out, but stopped halfway there. "Well I'll be."

Resting atop the chest of drawers the Necromancer had been rifling through was a good-sized strong box. Gareth stepped over to it, and found himself grinning. Maybe his luck was about to turn around. He forced the lock and flung the box open, and his grin grew even wider.

Gold always made him smile.

"Grab that, will you Hatherle?" He would not be able to carry it, wounded as he was. And besides, what was the point of having a man servant if not to have him lug things?

Hatherle sighed. As he picked up the strong box, he spoke in a tone of resignation, with perhaps a tiny bit of irritation beneath. "I am sworn to carry your burdens," he said.

Gareth shook his head in amusement.

He took a minute to pull flint and stone out of his belt pouch, then struck alight a few pieces of paper he found in the chest of drawers. He set the burning pages beneath the bed, and soon the bed was beginning to burn as well. With luck, maybe the entire place would go up. At the very least it would slow down the corpses' pursuit.

"Looks like we live to fight another day," he said.

Then he turned and hobbled down the stairs. Hatherle followed.

MESSAGE FROM THE AUTHOR

Thank you for reading my book. I hope you enjoyed reading it as much as I enjoyed writing it.

Every review helps an author out, so whether you loved this book, hated it, or something in between, please take a minute to tell other readers what you thought. All of the online retailers make it very easy to do, and I would really appreciate it.

Feel free to come say hi at my website or on Facebook. I always enjoy hearing from readers, especially since you all are, collectively, my boss.

I also have a weekly podcast, Story Time With Michael Kingswood, where I read stories and talk through some of the latest goings on in my world. I'd love to see you there.

Thanks again. My best to you and yours.

Warm Regards,
Michael Kingswood

MAILING LIST

If you enjoyed this book and would like word on new releases and special deals from Michael Kingswood, sign up for his newsletter on his website. Guaranteed to be spam-free, you can opt out at any time. And you can rest assured he will not share your information with anyone, for any reason.

https://michaelkingswood.com/newsletter-signup/

SUPPORTING PATRONAGE

Michael would like to invite you to become a supporting member of his website. Similar in concept to Patreon, a few dollars a month will give you access to exclusive content, and help him to focus more of his time to writing fun and exciting stories for your enjoyment.

Sign up at his website:

https://www.michaelkingswood.com/membership/supporting-patronage/

ABOUT THE AUTHOR

Michael Kingswood is 20-year veteran of the US Navy submarine force and a lifelong fan of science fiction and fantasy literature. His work has appeared in numerous collections and anthologies, to include the Fiction River Anthology series from WMG publishing. He holds a bachelors degree in Mechanical Engineering as well as a Master of Engineering Management and a Master of Business Administration. He has four children and currently resides in San Diego.

Find Michael Kingswood online at:

www.michaelkingswood.com

www.facebook.com/michael.kingswood

steemit.com/@michaelkingswood

Or on his Bitchute and Youtube Channels - Story Time With Michael Kingswood

MORE BOOKS BY MICHAEL KINGSWOOD

GLIMMER VALE CHRONICLES

Glimmer Vale

Out-Dweller

Tollard's Peak

Robbed Blind

Wedding Gifts: A Glimmer Vale Chronicles Story

The Falconer's Stairs

Glimmer Vale Omnibus Edition #1

THE PERICLES CONSPIRACY

Passing In The Night

The Pericles Conspiracy

DAWN OF ENLIGHTENMENT

Masters Of The Sun

NOVELLAS

What Lurks Between

The Necromancer's Lair

The Champion

Veritas Morte

STORY COLLECTIONS

Tales Of Adventure #1

Tales Of Adventure #2

Short Story 10-Pack

A Jar Of Mixed Treats

SHORT FICTION

Michael has also published a number of shorter works, links
to which can be found on his website.

www.ingramcontent.com/pod-product-compliance
Lightning Source LLC
Chambersburg PA
CBHW032050180726
48284CB00004B/1269